CICADA

SHAUN TAN

Hodder
Children's
Books

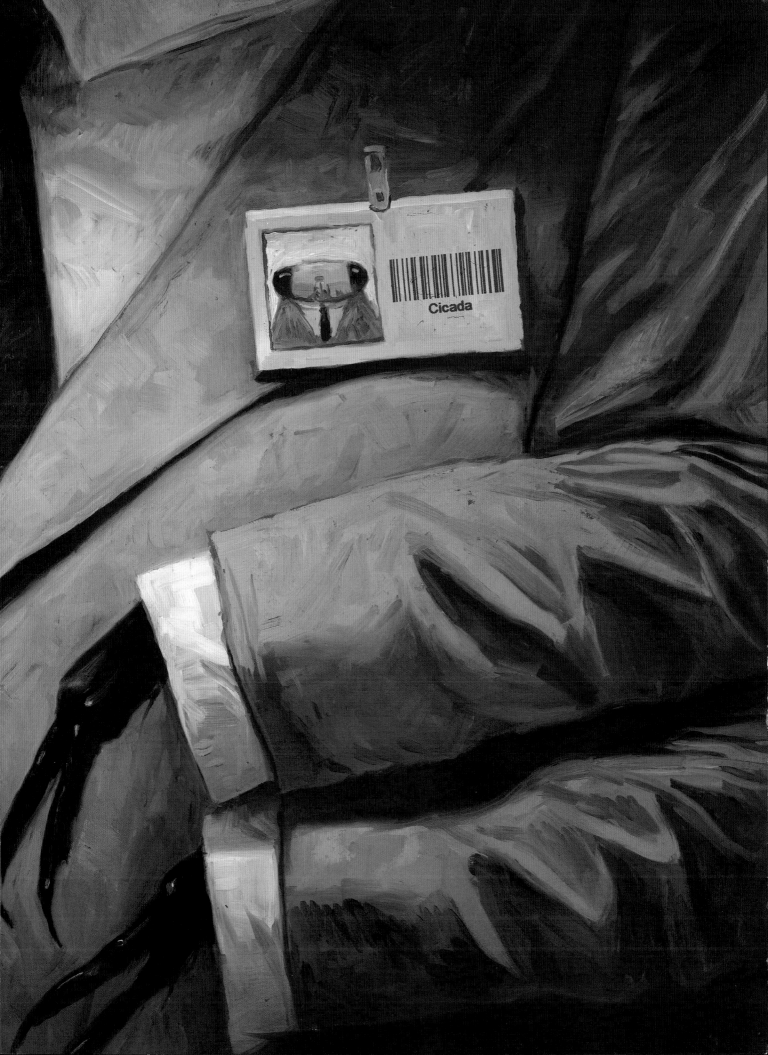

Cicada work in tall building.

Data entry clerk. Seventeen year.

No sick day. No mistake.

Tok Tok Tok!

Seventeen year. No promotion.

Human resources say cicada not human.

Need no resources.

Tok Tok Tok!

No cicada allowed in office bathroom.

Cicada go downtown. Twelve blocks.

Each time company dock pay.

Tok Tok Tok!

Human never finish work.

Cicada always stay late. Finish work.

Nobody thank cicada.

Tok Tok Tok!

Human coworker no like cicada.

Say things. Do things.

Think cicada stupid.

Tok Tok Tok!

Cicada no afford rent.

Live in office wallspace.

Company pretend not know.

Tok Tok Tok!

Seventeen year. Cicada retire.

No party. No handshake.

Boss say clean desk.

Tok Tok Tok!

No work. No home. No money.

Cicada go to top of tall building.

Time to say goodbye.

Tok Tok Tok!

Cicada all fly back to forest.

Sometimes think about human.

Can't stop laughing.

Tok Tok Tok!

閑かさや
岩にしみ入る
蝉の声

calm and serene
the sound of a cicada
penetrates the rock

Matsuo Bashō (1644–94)
trans. Yuzuru Miura

HODDER CHILDREN'S BOOKS
First published in Australia and New Zealand in 2018
by Lothian Children's Books, Hachette Australia
This edition first published in Great Britain in 2018 by Hodder and Stoughton

1 3 5 7 9 10 8 6 4 2

Text and illustrations copyright © Shaun Tan, 2018

ISBN 978 1 444 94620 8

Designed by Shaun Tan
Art photography by Matthew Stanton
Printed and bound in China

Hodder Children's Books
An imprint of Hachette Children's Group
Part of Hodder and Stoughton
Carmelite House, 50 Victoria Embankment, London, EC4Y 0DZ

An Hachette UK Company
www.hachette.co.uk

www.hachettechildrens.co.uk

Many thanks to Sophie Byrne, Helen Chamberlin, Inari Kiuru, Julia Adams,
Hilary Murray Hill, Anne McNeil, Emma Layfield, Paula Burgess, Christina Harrison,
Nicola Goode, Katy Cattell, Lucy Upton and the Hachette team.

Bashō haiku translation reprinted with permission from *Classic Haiku: A Master's*
Selection by Yuzuru Miura, published by Tuttle Publishing.